# SING NOEL

# Sing

Boyds Mills Press

Christmas Carols Selected by

# Jane Yolen

# Noel

MUSICAL ARRANGEMENTS BY

## Adam Stemple

ILLUSTRATIONS BY

## Nancy Sippel Carpenter

Text copyright © 1996 by Jane Yolen

Musical arrangements © 1996 by Adam Stemple

Illustrations copyright © 1996 by Nancy Sippel Carpenter

Published by Caroline House

Boyds Mills Press, Inc.

A Highlights Company

815 Church Street

Honesdale, Pennsylvania 18431

Printed in Mexico


Publisher Cataloging-in-Publication Data

Sing noel : Christmas carols / selected by Jane Yolen ; musical arrangements by Adam Stemple ;

illustrations by Nancy Sippel Carpenter. — 1st ed.

[96]p. : col. ill. ; cm.

Summary: A collection of traditional Christmas carols, including musical arrangements

and introductions that describe the history of each song.

ISBN 1-56397-420-7

1. Christmas music — Juvenile literature. 2. Carols — Collections — Juvenile literature.

[1. Christmas music. 2. Carols — Collections. 3. Songs — Christmas.]

1. Yolen, Jane. II. Stemple, Adam. III. Carpenter, Nancy Sippel, ill. IV. Title.

783.635 — dc20   1996   AC

Library of Congress Catalog Card Number 95-80770


First edition, 1996

Book designed by Joy Chu

The text of this book is set in 14-point Bernhard Modern; the song lyrics are set in 13-point Bernhard Modern;

with music in Petrucci.

The illustrations are watercolor with colored pencil.


10 9 8 7 6 5 4 3 2 1

For the STEMPLE COUSINS, who love Christmas —J.Y.

For JADE, LEXI, and BRENNAN RYAN —A.S.

For the SIPPEL CLAN —N.S.C.

# Contents

# Hark! the Herald Angels Sing

Charles Wesley (1707-1788), perhaps the best-known eighteenth-century writer of hymns and carols, was the eighteenth child born of a modest English family. A minister for a while, he lived in colonial Georgia. Dr. William Cummings set Wesley's words to a melody by German composer Felix Mendelssohn (1809-1847). The original Mendelssohn piece was written to commemorate the art of printing and had nothing at all to do with Christmas.

*Words by Charles Wesley*
*Music by Felix Mendelssohn*

Hark the her-ald an-gels sing,— "Glo-ry to the new-born King,

Peace on earth, and mer-cy mild,— God and sin-ners rec-on-ciled."

Joy - ful all ye na - tions rise,—— Join the tri - umph of the skies,——

With an - gel - ic hosts pro - claim, "Christ is— born in Beth - le - hem."

Hark! the her - ald an - gels sing, "Glo - ry—— to the new - born King."

# Jingle Bells

James Pierpont (1822-1893) wrote this popular Christmas carol in 1857. A "bobtail" is a horse whose tail has been bobbed, or cut short.

*With a bounce*

*Words and music by James Pierpont*

1. Dash-ing through the snow in a one-horse o-pen sleigh, O'er the fields we go,

*continued*

2. A day or two ago
   I thought I'd take a ride,
   And soon Miss Fannie Bright
   Was seated by my side.
   The horse was lean and lank;
   Misfortune seemed his lot;
   He got into a drifted bank
   And we, we got up-sot.
   (chorus)

3. Now the ground is white;
   Go it while you're young;
   Take the girls tonight,
   And sing this sleighing song.
   Just get a bobtailed bay,
   Two-forty as his speed;
   Hitch him to an open sleigh,
   And, crack, you'll take the lead.
   (chorus)

# Masters in This Hall

William Morris (1834-1896)—writer, painter, designer—
penned the words to this carol shortly before 1860. The tune he set
them to was an old French carol.

Words by William Morris
Music French traditional

*Brightly*

1. Mas-ters in this hall, _____ Hear ye news to - day, _____ Brought from o - ver sea _____ And ev - er I you pray:
2. Go - ing o'er the hills, _____ Thro' the milk-white snow, _____ Heard I ew - es bleat, _____ While the wind did blow.

*continued*

*(chorus)* No-el! No-el! No - el! No - el sing we clear! Hol - pen

are all folks on earth. Born is God's Son so dear.

No - el! No - el! No - el! No - el sing we loud! God to-

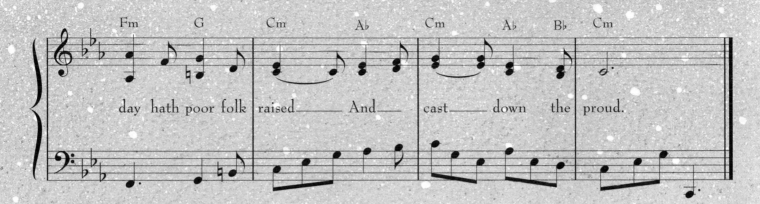

day hath poor folk raised_____ And_____ cast_____ down the proud.

3. Then to Bethlehem town
   We went two by two,
   And in a sorry place
   Heard the oxen low:
   *(chorus)*

4. Therein did we see
   A sweet and goodly may
   And a fair old man,
   Upon the straw she lay:
   *(chorus)*

5. And a little Child
   On her arm had she.
   "Wot ye who this is?"
   Said the hinds to me:
   *(chorus)*

6. "This is Christ the Lord,
   Masters be ye glad!
   Christmas is come in,
   And no folks should be sad":
   *(chorus)*

# The Friendly Beasts

This twelfth-century English poem originated as a medieval mystery play and later became part of the Christmas pageants performed by local guild members. The tune is from Beauvais, France, part of the "Fête de l'Âne" ("The Donkey's Festival"), another medieval Christmas extravaganza.

Words English traditional
Music French traditional

Gently

1. Je - sus our broth - er, kind and good, Was
2. "I," said the don - key, shaggy and brown, "I

hum - bly born in a sta - ble rude, And the
carried His Moth - er up hill and down; I___

friend - ly    beasts        a - round      Him      stood;
carried   her   safely    to      Beth - l'hem    town.

Je - sus,  our      broth - er,       kind    and    good.
I,"   said  the      don - key,       shaggy  and    brown.

3. "I," said the cow, all white and red,
   "I gave Him my manger for His bed;
   I gave Him my hay to pillow His head;
   I," said the cow, all white and red.

4. "I," said the sheep with curly horn,
   "I gave Him my wool for His blanket warm.
   He wore my coat on Christmas morn.
   I," said the sheep with curly horn.

5. "I," said the dove from the rafters high,
   "I cooed Him to sleep that He should not cry.
   We cooed Him to sleep, my mate and I.
   I," said the dove from the rafters high.

6. Thus every beast by some good spell,
   In the stable dark was glad to tell
   Of the gift he gave Emmanuel,
   The gift he gave Emmanuel.

## Angels We Have Heard on High

The Latin hymn "Gloria in Excelsis Deo" was first sung in A.D. 129 as part of the Christmas observance by order of the Roman bishop Telesphorus, and so it was the very first Christmas carol. It was known for years as the "Angel's Hymn." We sing a very different form of it today. The chorus of this popular carol is only a small part of that long-ago hymn.

*Gloria in excelsis Deo* means "Glory to God in the highest."

With majesty        Traditional

1. An-gels we have heard on high, Sweet-ly sing-ing o'er the plains,

And the moun-tains in re-ply, Ech-o-ing their joy-ous strains:

*continued*

20

D7      G Am G C     G     D7     G

*- ri - a    in ex - cel - sis    De -    o.*

2. Shepherds, why this jubilee?
   Why your joyous strains prolong?
   What the gladsome tidings be
   Which inspire your heav'nly song?
   *(chorus)*

3. Come to Bethlehem and see
   Him whose birth the angels sing;
   Come, adore on bended knee,
   Christ the Lord, the newborn King.
   *(chorus)*

4. See Him in a manger laid,
   Whom the choirs of angels praise;
   Mary, Joseph, lend your aid,
   While our hearts in love we raise.
   *(chorus)*

# Away in a Manger

This song was long attributed to the great theologian Martin Luther. But in fact it was written by American composer William James Kirkpatrick (1838-1921), who directed church music for his Sunday-school class. It was first printed in Philadelphia in 1885.

*Tenderly*

*Words and music by William James Kirkpatrick*

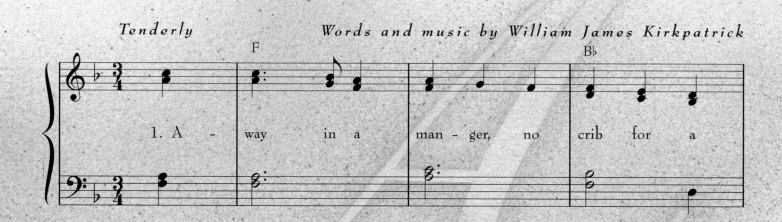

1. A - way in a man - ger, no crib for a

bed. The lit - tle Lord Je - sus lay down His sweet

head. The stars in the sky— looked down where He

lay, The lit - tle Lord Je - sus a - sleep in the hay.

2. The cattle are lowing, the Baby awakes,
   But little Lord Jesus no crying He makes.
   I love Thee, Lord Jesus! Look down from the sky,
   And stay by my side until morning is nigh.

3. Be near me, Lord Jesus; I ask Thee to stay
   Close by me forever, and love me, I pray.
   Bless all the dear children in Thy tender care,
   And fit us for heaven, to live with Thee there.

# The Boar's Head Carol

The oldest English carol still sung regularly, this song was published in Wynken de Worde's *Christmasse Carols* in 1521. It was part of the traditional Christmas festival at Queen's College and chanted while a boar's head was carried in procession to the table. The serving of the boar's head—so legend goes—started when an Oxford student was walking in the hills near his college and a wild boar rushed at him. He thrust his book of Aristotle's teachings down the boar's throat, killing it, and his friends served up the wild pig in thanksgiving.

*In a stately manner*

English traditional

1. The boar's head in hand bear I, be - decked with bay and rose-mar-y. And I
2. The boar's head, I un - der-stand, Is the fin - est dish in all the land. Which

pray you, my mas - ters be mer - ry, *Quot est - is in con - vi - vi - o.*
thus be - decked with a gay gar - land, Let us *ser - vi - re can - ti-co.*

*(chorus)*

*Ca - put a - pri de - fer - o, Red - dens lau - des Dom - i - no.*

25

# Born Is Jesus, the Infant King

A French carol known as "Il Est Né, le Divin Enfant," this song was a favorite of the famous Trapp family singers.

*Merrily*

*French traditional*

(chorus) Born is Je- sus, the In- fant King, Play—mer-ry o-boes sweet pipes re - sound - ing;

Born is Je - sus, the In- fant King, Come His Ad- vent on earth to sing!

More than four thou-sand years' de-lay, Since the pro-phets of God fore-told Him.
Ah, how fair is the Child we sing, How de-light-ful—— to be-hold Him.

More than four thou-sand years' de-lay Passed be-fore this all joy-ful day.
Ah, how fair is the Child we sing, He is love-ly, the In-fant King!

# Pat-a-Pan

This carol comes from Burgundy, a region in France, and recalls the custom of music making in medieval towns at Christmastime.

*With spirit*                                                                                                   *French traditional*

Chil - dren bring your flute and drum, For the jol - ly time has

# Christmas Is Coming

This is an old English song that can be sung as a three-part round. In Europe and Great Britain, goose is the traditional holiday meal.

# O Come, O Come, Emmanuel

T̲he earliest carol still sung today, this song was originally a Gregorian chant in Latin. The translation used here is by John Mason Neale (1818-1866), who wrote the words to "Good King Wenceslas."

*English translation by John Mason Neale*
*Music traditional*

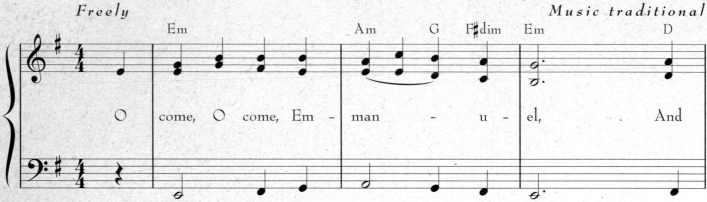

O come, O come, Em - man - u - el, And

ran - som cap - tive Is - ra - el, That mourns in lone - ly

# Deck the Halls

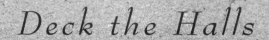

*T*his popular carol comes from Wales. It is sung in the style of
madrigals, which were popular in England during the late
sixteenth century. These madrigals had a refrain
following each line of the verse.

*Brightly*                                           *Welsh traditional*

1. Deck the halls with boughs of hol – ly, Fa la la la la, la la la la.

'Tis the sea – son to be jol – ly, Fa la la la la, la la la la.

Don we now our gay ap – par – el, Fa la la la, la la la, la la la.

Troll the an – cient Yule – tide car – ol, Fa la la la la, la la la la.

2. See the blazing Yule before us,
Fa la la la la, la la la la.
Strike the harp and join the chorus,
Fa la la la la, la la la la.
Follow me in merry measure,
Fa la la la, la la la, la la la,
While I tell of Yuletide treasure,
Fa la la la la, la la la la.

3. Fast away the old year passes,
Fa la la la la, la la la la.
Hail the new, ye lads and lasses,
Fa la la la la, la la la la.
Sing we joyous all together,
Fa la la la, la la la, la la la,
Heedless of the wind and weather,
Fa la la la la, la la la la.

# Carol of the Birds

The words of this traditional song are attributed to
Bas-Quercy. Birds often figure in Christmas stories.
"Philomel" is the poetic name for the nightingale.

Words by Bas-Quercy
Music French traditional

With emotion

1. Whence comes this rush of wings a - far, Fol - low - ing straight the No - el star?
2. "Tell us, ye birds, why come ye here, In - to this sta - ble, poor and drear?"

Birds from the woods in won - drous flight, Beth - le - hem seek this ho - ly night.
"Hast - 'ning we seek the new - born King, And all our sweet - est mu - sic bring."

36

3. Hark! how the greenfinch bears his part,
Philomel, too, with tender heart,
Chants from her leafy dark retreat,
Re, mi, fa, sol, in accents sweet.

4. Angels and shepherds, birds of the sky,
Come where the Son of God doth lie;
Christ on earth with man doth dwell,
Join in the shout, "Noel, Noel!"

# It Came Upon the Midnight Clear

The Unitarian minister Edmund Hamilton Sears lived from 1810-1876.
He wrote the words to this carol in 1850, and the next year the composer
Richard S. Willis (1819-1900) set them to music.

*Words by Edmund Hamilton Sears*
*Music by Richard S. Willis*

1. It came up-on the mid-night clear, That glo-rious song of old, From an-gels bend-ing near the earth To touch their harps of old,
2. Still thro' the clo-ven skies they come, With peace-ful wings un-furled; And still their heav-en-ly mu-sic floats O'er all the wea-ry

# O Christmas Tree

**A**lso known by its German title, "O Tannenbaum," this song harkens back to the custom of decorating the Christmas tree, a tradition that originally came from Germany.

*Flowingly*

*German traditional*

O Christ - mas tree, O Christ - mas tree, For - ev - er green thy branch - es. O Christ - mas tree, O Christ - mas tree, For - ev - er green thy

branch - es.   Not on - ly green   in   sum - mer's glow,   But   green as well   in

win - ter's snow.   O   Christ - mas tree, O   Christ - mas tree, For - ev - er green thy   branch - es.

## O Little Town of Bethlehem

In 1868, after a visit to Bethlehem, a Philadelphia minister named Phillips Brooks (1835-1893) wrote the words to this carol. He gave the little poem to the church organist, Lewis H. Redner, hoping to have the song ready for the Sunday-school children to sing for Christmas. Redner put off writing the tune until the Saturday before it was due. Roused from sleep by the strains whispering in his ear, Redner jotted down the melody line and fell back to sleep. When he awoke Sunday morning, he quickly filled in the harmony just in time for the children of the Episcopal Church of the Holy Trinity in Philadelphia to sing it for the first time. When the song was published in a Massachusetts Sunday-school hymn book, it began its journey into the hearts of children everywhere.

Words by Phillips Brooks
Music by Lewis H. Redner

Lovingly

1. O lit - tle town of Beth - le - hem, How still we— see thee lie. A - bove thy deep and dream-less sleep The si - lent— stars go


continued

43

2. For Christ is born of Mary;
   And gathered all above,
   While mortals sleep, the angels keep
   Their watch of wondering love.
   O morning stars together
   Proclaim the holy birth;
   And praises sing to God the King,
   And peace to men on earth.

3. How silently, how silently,
   The wondrous gift is given!
   So God imparts to human hearts
   The blessings of His heaven.
   No ear may hear His coming;
   But in this world of sin,
   Where meek souls will receive Him, still
   The dear Christ enters in.

4. O Holy Child of Bethlehem,
   Descend to us, we pray;
   Cast out our sin and enter in;
   Be born in us today.
   We hear the Christmas angels
   The great glad tidings tell;
   O come to us, abide with us,
   Our Lord Emmanuel.

45

# Ding Dong! Merrily on High

The English words of this song were written by G. R. Woodward and grafted to a merry sixteenth-century French dance tune. The dance was called a "branle." It had two heavy beats, on which the dancers jumped into the air with their feet together.

Words by G. R. Woodward
Music French traditional

*Happily*

1. Ding dong! Mer-ri-ly on high In heav'n the bells are ring - ing,

Ding dong! Ver-i-ly the sky Is riv'n with an - gel sing - ing.

(chorus) Glo - - - - - - - ri - a, Ho - san - na in ex - cel - sis.

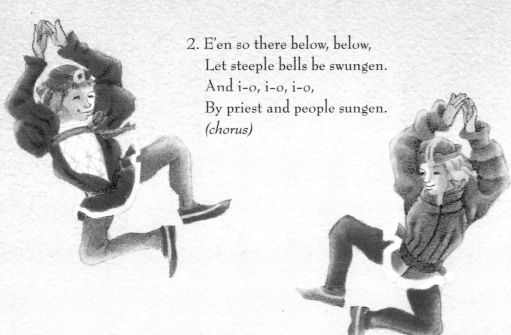

2. E'en so there below, below,
   Let steeple bells be swungen.
   And i-o, i-o, i-o,
   By priest and people sungen.
   (chorus)

3. Pray you, dutifully prime
   Your matin chime, ye ringers;
   May you beautifully rime
   Your evening song, ye singers.
   (chorus)

# The First Noel

There is disagreement over whether this was originally a French or an English carol, but this medieval shepherd's song is certainly one of the oldest carols still popular today.

continued

2. They looked up and saw a star
   Shining in the East beyond them far,
   And to the earth it gave great light,
   And so it continued both day and night.
   *(chorus)*

3. This star drew nigh to the northwest,
   O'er Bethlehem it took its rest.
   And there it did both stop and stay
   Right over the place where Jesus lay.
   *(chorus)*

4. Then enter'd in those wise men three,
   Full rev'rently upon their knee,
   And offer'd there in His presence,
   Their gold and myrrh and frankincense.
   *(chorus)*

5. Then let us all with one accord
   Sing praises to our heavenly Lord,
   That hath made heaven and earth of nought,
   And with His blood mankind hath bought.
   *(chorus)*

# Here We Come A-Wassailing

Waes Hael or Wes Hal is the old Anglo-Saxon toast meaning "be in health." It was sung by the Saxons to their lords at traditional feasts. The custom of going wassailing is an English one in which children—sometimes with blackened faces—go door to door on Christmas Eve carrying evergreens and singing. The words of this particular song date from the seventeenth century.

Joyously

1. ___ Here we come a - was - sail - ing A - mong the leaves so

green. ___ Here we come a - wan - d'ring So fair ___ to be seen.

(chorus) Love and joy come to you, And to you your was - sail,

continued

too, And God bless you and send you a Hap — py New Year, And God send you a Hap — py New Year.

2. We are not daily beggars
   Who beg from door to door,
   But we are neighbors' children
   Whom you have seen before.
   (*chorus*)

3. God bless the master of this house,
   Likewise the mistress, too;
   And all the little children
   That round the table go.
   (*chorus*)

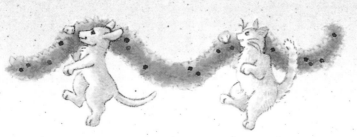

# God Rest You Merry, Gentlemen

The lyrics to this traditional English carol have been sung to
at least two different tunes over the past three hundred years. The most
popular tune, the one used in this book, was first printed and sold in
London in the 1790s. In the fourth verse, the word "friends" is thought by
some scholars to be a misprint for the word "fiends." So take your pick.

*continued*

day. To save us all from Sa-tan's power When we were gone a-

stray; O——— tid - ings of com - fort and joy, com-fort and

joy. O——— tid - ings of com - fort and joy.

2. In Bethlehem in Jewry
   This blessèd Babe was born,
   And laid within a manger
   Upon this blessèd morn;
   The which His Mother, Mary,
   Did nothing take in scorn:
   *(chorus)*

3. From God our heavenly Father
   A blessèd angel came,
   And unto certain shepherds
   Brought tidings of the same,
   How that in Bethlehem was born
   The Son of God by name:
   *(chorus)*

4. "Fear not," then said the angel,
   "Let nothing you afright,
   This day is born a Savior
   Of virtue, power, and might;
   So frequently to vanquish all
   The friends of Satan quite":
   *(chorus)*

5. The shepherds at those tidings
   Rejoicèd much in mind,
   And left their flocks a-feeding
   In tempest, storm, and wind,
   And went to Bethlehem straightway
   This blessèd Babe to find:
   *(chorus)*

6. But when to Bethlehem they came,
   Whereat this Infant lay,
   They found Him in a manger
   Where oxen feed on hay,
   His Mother, Mary, kneeling
   Unto the Lord did pray:
   *(chorus)*

7. Now to the Lord sing praises,
   All you within this place,
   And with true love and brotherhood
   Each other now embrace;
   This holy tide of Christmas
   All others doth deface:
   *(chorus)*

# We Wish You a Merry Christmas

This English carol is full of good cheer as it recalls the carolers who go from door to door and are rewarded for their good singing with figgy pudding— a traditional English plum pudding served at Christmas—or a hot drink.

*Merrily*

*English traditional*

1. We wish you a Mer–ry Christ–mas, We wish you a Mer–ry Christ–mas, We wish you a Mer–ry Christ–mas and a Hap–py New Year. *(chorus)* Glad

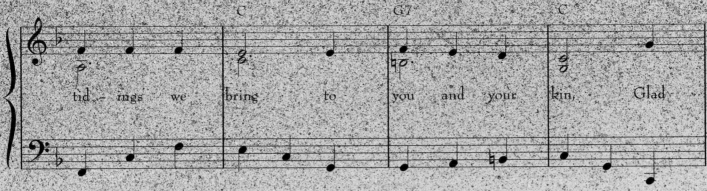

tid - ings we bring to you and your kin, Glad

tid - ings for Christ - mas and a Hap - py New Year.

2. Now bring us some figgy pudding,
   Now bring us some figgy pudding,
   Now bring us some figgy pudding,
   And a cup of good cheer.
   *(chorus)*

3. We won't go until we get some,
   We won't go until we get some,
   We won't go until we get some,
   So bring it right here!
   *(chorus)*

# Angels from the Realms of Glory

Hymn writer James Montgomery (1771-1854), a minister of the Moravian Brethren, wrote the words of this song using the old French carol "Les Anges dans Nos Campagnes" as a basis. Though the poem was completed in 1816 and had several different musical settings, it was not until Henry Smart (1813-1879) wrote this tune for it in 1867 that the carol became a special Christmas favorite.

*Words by James Montgomery*
*Music by Henry Smart*

1. An - gels from the realms of glo - ry Wing your flight o'er all the earth; Ye who sang cre - a - tion's sto - ry,

2. Shep - herds in the fields a - bid - ing, Watch - ing o'er your flocks by night; God with man is now re - sid - ing,

Amin   E   Amin              G    D7    G         (chorus)

Now pro - claim Mes - si - ah's birth;
Yon - der shines the___ In - fant Light;
Come and wor - ship,

C            F          Dmin   C  G(Bbass) Am    D7   G   C

Come and wor - ship, Wor - ship Christ, the new - born King.

# The Seven Joys of Mary

There are many English and American versions of this carol. The text goes back to the fifteenth-century mystery plays in England, but it bears a strong resemblance to other counting songs that can be traced back to the pre-Christian era and the Jewish tradition.

*With a bit of a bounce*　　　　　　　　　　　　　　　*English traditional*

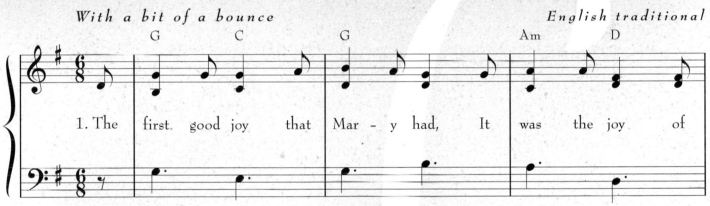

1. The first good joy that Mar - y had, It was the joy of

one;＿＿ To see the bless - èd Je - sus Christ, When He was first＿ her

*continued*

Son.——— When He was first her Son, Good Lord— And hap - py may we

be;— Praise Fa - ther, Son, and Ho - ly Ghost To all e - ter - ni - ty.———

2. The next good joy that Mary had,
   It was the joy of two;
   To see her own Son, Jesus Christ,
   Making the lame to go.
   Making the lame to go, Good Lord,
   (chorus)

3. The next good joy that Mary had,
   It was the joy of three;
   To see her own Son, Jesus Christ,
   Making the blind to see.
   Making the blind to see, Good Lord,
   (chorus)

4. The next good joy that Mary had,
   It was the joy of four;
   To see her own Son, Jesus Christ,
   Reading the Bible o'er.
   Reading the Bible o'er, Good Lord,
   (chorus)

5. The next good joy that Mary had,
   It was the joy of five;
   To see her own Son, Jesus Christ,
   Raising the dead to life.
   Raising the dead to life, Good Lord,
   (chorus)

6. The next good joy that Mary had,
   It was the joy of six;
   To see her own Son, Jesus Christ,
   Upon the Crucifix.
   Upon the Crucifix, Good Lord,
   (chorus)

7. The next good joy that Mary had,
   It was the joy of seven;
   To see her own Son, Jesus Christ,
   Ascending into heaven.
   Ascending into heaven, Good Lord,
   (chorus)

# The Coventry Carol

*I*n the Middle Ages, craft guilds often performed elaborate pageants at Christmas with songs and dances and plays. This carol was part of one such performance by the Shearman and Tailors Guild of Coventry, England, in 1534.

*With emotion*　　　　　　　　　　　　　　　　　　　　　　*English traditional*

1. Lul - ly, lul - lay, Thou ti - ny Child,

Bye - bye, lul - ly, lul - lay._____ Lul-

ly,    lul - lay,    Thou    ti - ny    Child,

Bye-bye, lul - ly,    lul - lay.    lay.

2. O sisters too,
   How may we do
   For to preserve this day;
   This poor Youngling
   For whom we sing
   Bye-bye, lully, lullay.

3. Herod, the king,
   In his raging
   Chargèd he hath this day
   His men of might
   In his own sight
   All children young to slay.

4. Then woe is me,
   Poor Child, for Thee,
   And ever mourn and say:
   For Thy parting
   Neither say nor sing,
   Bye-bye, lully, lullay.

# Good King Wenceslas

In 1853 John Mason Neale (1818-1866) wrote a poem about the famous tenth-century King Wenzel of Bohemia, who was celebrated for his many kind acts to benefit the poor. Dr. Neale set the poem to a thirteenth-century dance carol found in *Piae Cantiones*, a Latin hymn book. The lyrics of that song originally went something like "The time of flowers is at hand / For the flowers are springing up." Since the Feast of St. Stephen is on December 26 and it is usually quite snowy in Bohemia then, there is nothing to relate the poem and music excepting Dr. Neale's genius, with hefty help from a song and dance team of the day that popularized the tune.

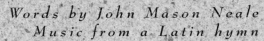

Words by John Mason Neale
Music from a Latin hymn

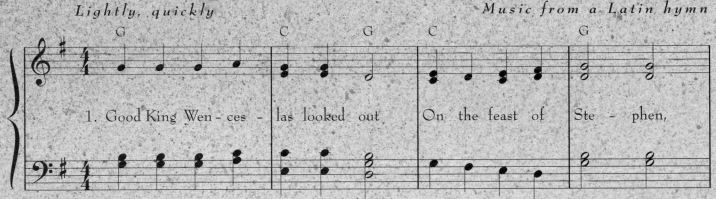

Lightly, quickly

1. Good King Wen - ces - las looked out On the feast of Ste - phen,

When the snow lay round a - bout, Deep and crisp and e - ven.

continued

Bright-ly shone the moon that night, Though the frost was cru - el,

When a poor man came in sight Gath-'ring win - ter fu - el.

2. "Hither, page, and stand by me,
   If thou know'st it, telling,
   Yonder peasant, who is he?
   Where and what his dwelling?"
   "Sire, he lives a good league hence,
   Underneath the mountain,
   Right against the forest fence,
   By Saint Agnes' fountain."

3. "Bring me flesh, and bring me wine,
   Bring me pine logs hither:
   Thou and I will see him dine,
   When we bear them thither."
   Page and monarch, forth they went,
   Forth they went together;
   Through the rude wind's wild lament
   And the bitter weather.

4. "Sire, the night is darker now,
   And the wind blows stronger;
   Fails my heart, I know not how;
   I can go no longer."
   "Mark my footsteps, my good page;
   Tread thou in them boldly:
   Thou shalt find the winter's rage
   Freeze thy blood less coldly."

5. In his master's steps he trod,
   Where the snow lay dinted;
   Heat was in the very sod
   Which the Saint had printed.
   Therefore, Christian men, be sure,
   Wealth or rank possessing,
   Ye who now will bless the poor,
   Shall yourselves find blessing.

71

# Joy to the World

The words of this carol are by the great English hymn writer Isaac Watts (1674-1748) and published in his *Psalms of David*. It is a paraphrase of Psalm 98 in the Old Testament: "Shout unto the Lord, all the earth . . ." The poem first appeared in print in 1839 and was later put to music that was very similar to a George Frederick Handel tune by the American composer and educator Lowell Mason (1792-1872).

*Words by Isaac Watts*
*Music by Lowell Mason*

With spirit

1. Joy to the world! the Lord is come; Let

heav - en____ and    heav - en and    na - ture    sing.

2. Joy to the world! the Savior reigns;
   Let men their songs employ;
   While fields and floods, rocks, hills, and plains
   Repeat the sounding joy,
   Repeat the sounding joy,
   Repeat, repeat the sounding joy.

3. No more let sin and sorrow grow,
   Nor thorns infest the ground;
   He comes to make His blessings flow
   Far as the curse is found,
   Far as the curse is found,
   Far as, far as the curse is found.

4. He rules the world with truth and grace,
   And makes the nations prove
   The glories of His righteousness,
   And wonders of His love,
   And wonders of His love,
   And wonders, and wonders of His love.

# O Come, All Ye Faithful

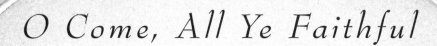

**A**lso known by its Latin name, "Adeste Fideles," this carol was written in Latin by the English music teacher John Francis Wade (1711-1786?) in the eighteenth century and later translated by the Reverend Frederick Oakeley (1802-1880) in the nineteenth century. The words were first published in 1760 in *Evening Offices of the Church,* and not until twenty-two years later was the tune printed. The carol was not originally intended as a joyous holiday song for everyone to sing, but rather as part of a church service.

*Latin words by*
*John Francis Wade*
*English translation by*
*Reverend Frederick Oakeley*
*Music by John Reading*

Moderately

1. O come, all ye faith - ful, joy - ful and tri-

Continued

dore Him, O come, let us a - dore Him,____ Christ,____ the Lord.

2. Sing, choirs of angels, sing in exultation,
   Sing, all ye citizens of heav'n above:
   Glory to God, in the highest:
   *(chorus)*

3. Yea Lord, we greet Thee, born this happy morning,
   Jesus, to Thee be glory giv'n;
   Word of the Father, now in flesh appearing:
   *(chorus)*

Latin (first verse):
*Adeste fideles, laeti triumphantes;*
*Venite, venite in Bethlehem.*
*Natum videte, Regem angelorum;*
*Venite adoremus,*
*Venite adoremus,*
*Venite adoremus Dominum.*

# Lo, How a Rose E'er Blooming

Written by the German composer Michael Praetorius (1571–1621), this carol is a favorite of choirs at Christmas.

*With great emotion*

*Words and music by Michael Praetorius*

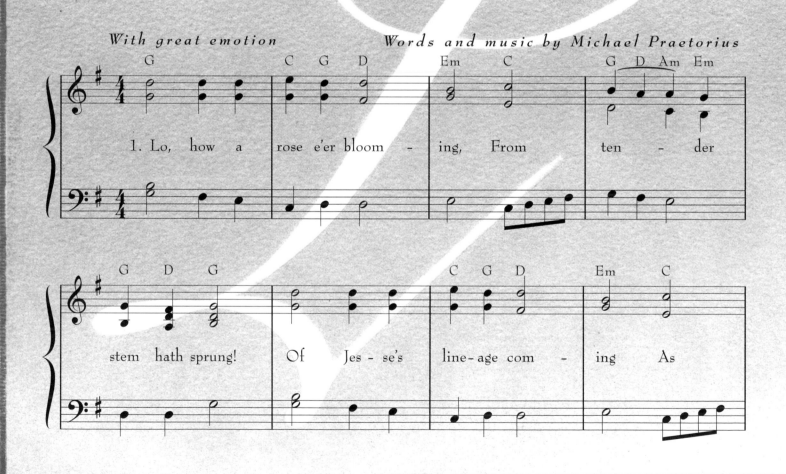

1. Lo, how a rose e'er bloom - ing, From ten - der stem hath sprung! Of Jes - se's line-age com - ing As

men___ of___ old have sung. It came, a flow'r - et bright, A - mid the cold of win - ter, When___ half spent was the night.

2. Isaiah 'twas foretold it,
   The rose I have in mind,
   With Mary we behold it,
   The Virgin Mother kind.
   To show God's love aright
   She bore to men a Savior,
   When half spent was the night.

# The Cherry Tree Carol

This is only one of many different melodies to which "The Cherry Tree Carol" is sung in both America and Great Britain. The story is one of the old miracle tales, though whether the story or the song came first is not clear.

*Charmingly*                                                                                      *Traditional*

1. Jo - seph was an old___ man, An old man was___
Jo - seph and Mar - y were walk - ing one___

he; He mar - ried Vir - gin Mar - y, The___
day, "Here are ap - ples and___ cher - ries," Sweet___

Queen of___ Gal – i – lee.
Mar – y___ did___

2. As    say.

3. Then Mary said to Joseph,
   So meek and so mild,
   "Joseph, gather me some cherries,
   For I am with Child."

4. Then Joseph flew in anger,
   In anger flew he,
   "Let the father of the Baby
   Gather cherries for thee."

5. Jesus spoke a few words,
   A few words spoke He,
   "Give My Mother some cherries,
   Bow down, cherry tree!

6. "Bow down, cherry tree,
   Low down to the ground."
   Then Mary gathered cherries,
   And Joseph stood around.

7. Then Joseph took Mary
   All on his right knee,
   "What have I done, Lord?
   Have mercy on me."

8. Then Joseph took Mary
   All on his left knee,
   "Oh, tell me, little Baby,
   When Thy birthday will be."

9. "The sixth of January
   My birthday will be,
   When the stars in the elements
   Will tremble with glee."

# I Heard the Bells on Christmas Day

At the height of the Civil War in America, poet Henry Wadsworth Longfellow (1807–1882) penned this poem, which rings with both despair and joy. He finished it on Christmas Day, 1863. It was later put to music by the prolific British composer J. Baptiste Calkin. It is the best known of his many pieces of church music and hymns.

*Words by Henry Wadsworth Longfellow*
*Music by J. Baptiste Calkin*

*Lyrically*

1. I heard the bells on Christ - mas Day, Their old fa - mil - iar

Gmin    C7                                          F

car - ols play, And   wild   and sweet the   words   re-peat Of   peace on earth, good

1.
C7                F        2.    C7                F

will        to   men.    will        to   men.

2.  I thought how, as the day had come,
    The belfries of all Christendom
    Had roll'd along th' unbroken song
    Of peace on earth, good will to men.

3. And in despair I bow'd my head:
   "There is no peace on earth," I said,
   "For hate is strong and mocks the song
   Of peace on earth, good will to men."

4. Then pealed the bells more loud and deep:
   "God is not dead, nor doth He sleep;
   The wrong shall fail, the right prevail,
   With peace on earth, good will to men."

5. Till, ringing, singing on its way
   The world revolv'd from night to day,
   A voice, a chime, a chant sublime,
   Of peace on earth, good will to men!

# We Three Kings of Orient Are

An American Christmas carol, this song was written by minister John H. Hopkins Jr. (1795-1873) in 1857. He used the St. Matthew's version of the Christmas story, which includes the three wise kings, or magi, from the Orient.

*Steadily*

*Words and music by John H. Hopkins Jr.*

1. We three kings of O - ri - ent are,

Bear - ing gifts we tra - verse a - far.

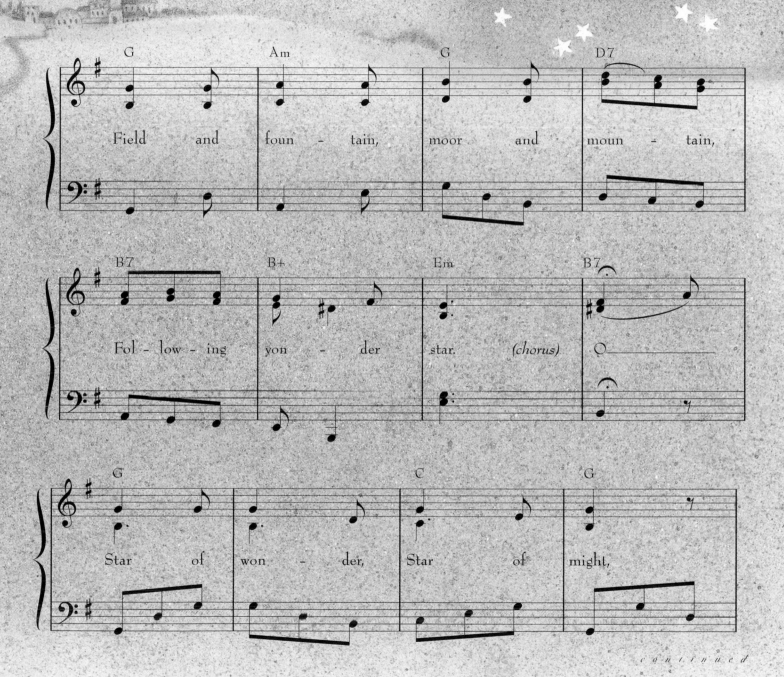

*continued*

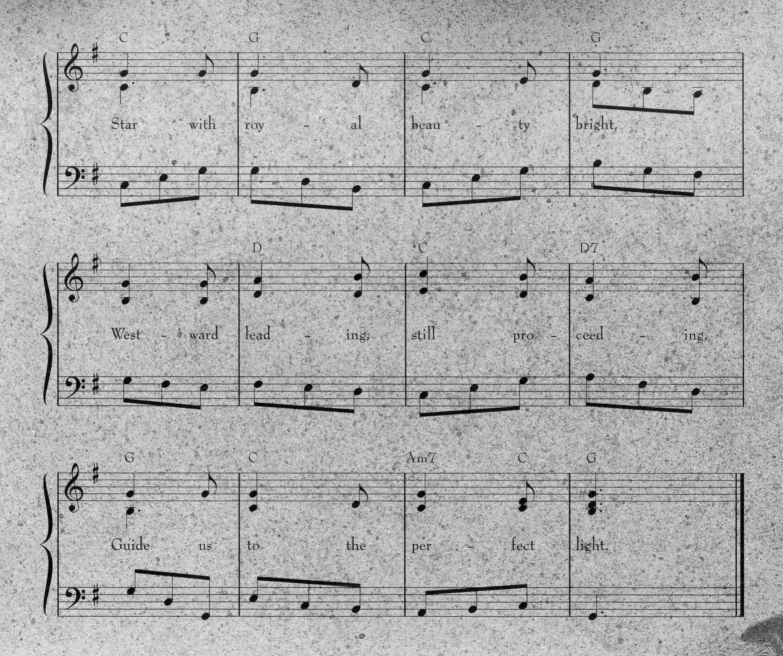

2. Born a Babe on Bethlehem's plain,
   Gold we bring to crown Him again;
   King forever, ceasing never,
   Over us all to reign.
   *(chorus)*

3. Frankincense to offer have I;
   Incense owns a Deity nigh,
   Pray'r and praising all men raising,
   Worship God on high.
   *(chorus)*

4. Myrrh is mine; its bitter perfume
   Breathes a life of gath'ring gloom;
   Sorrowing, sighing, bleeding, dying,
   Sealed in the stone-cold tomb.
   *(chorus)*

5. Glorious now behold Him rise,
   King and God and sacrifice;
   Heav'n sings "Hallelujah!"
   "Hallelujah!" earth replies.
   *(chorus)*

# Bring a Torch, Jeannette Isabella

*T*his traditional French carol is from the region of Provence. Sometimes the translation is sung "Torches here, Jeannette Isabella."

*Sweetly*

*French traditional*

1. Bring a torch,— Jean - nette Is - a - bel - la! Bring a torch, to the cra - dle run! He is here,— good

folk of the vil – lage; Christ— is born and Mar – y's

call – ing: Ah! Ah! Beau – ti – ful is the Moth – er!

continued

Ah! Ah! Beau - ti - ful is the Child.____

2. Wrong it is, when the Baby is sleeping,
   Wrong it is to shout so loud.
   Now you there, and you others, be quiet!
   For at a sound our Jesus wakens.
   Hush! Hush! Hush! He is sleeping soundly.
   Hush! Hush! Hush! do but see Him sleep.

3. Who comes there in this way knocking, knocking?
   Who comes there knocking, knocking like that?
   Open then! We have put on a plate
   Some very good cakes, which here we carry,
   *Toc! toc! toc!* open wide the door then,
   *Toc! toc! toc!* let us have a feast!

4. Softly now in the narrow stable,
   Softly now for a moment stay.
   Come quite near! How charming is Jesus!
   Oh, look, how white! Oh, see, how rosy!
   Do! do! do! let the Baby slumber!
   Do! do! do! see the Baby smile!

# Rise Up, Shepherd, and Follow

**A**n African American slave song, this popular carol has many variations, as it was passed down orally through the years.

*Strongly*  
*American traditional*

1. There's a star in the East on— Christ-mas morn, Rise up, shep-herd, and fol-low; It will lead to the place where the Sav-ior's born,— Rise up, shep-herd, and fol-low.

2. If you take good heed to an an-gel's words You'll for-get your flocks, you'll for-get your herds,— Rise up, shep-herd, and fol-low.

*continued*

# Silent Night

Two days before Christmas in 1818, the organ bellows of St. Nikolas Church in Oberndorf, Austria, had worn out, rotted by the frequent flooding of the Salzach River. Fearing there would be no music for Christmas Eve Mass, the young parish priest, Father Josef Mohr (1792-1848), wrote the words of this tender song. He asked Franz Gruber (1787-1863), the church organist, to write the music. That night, with Gruber singing the bass line and playing the guitar and Mohr singing the tenor, the song was heard for the first time on Christmas Eve. But Mohr was transferred to another church the next year and lost touch with Gruber. In 1825 Carl Mauracher was hired to rebuild the church organ, and he found a handwritten copy of the song in the organ loft. He took it home with him and played it for friends. The song became part of the singing repertory of the concert troupe The Strasser Children, who toured around Europe. It was said to be a favorite of King Friedrich Wilhelm IV of Prussia.

*Words by Father Josef Mohr*
*Music by Franz Gruber*

*Tenderly*

1. Si - lent night! Ho - ly night! All is calm, all is bright.

2. Silent night! Holy night!
   Shepherds quake at the sight!
   Glories stream from heaven afar,
   Heav'nly hosts sing "Alleluia!"
   Christ, the Savior, is born!
   Christ, the Savior, is born!

3. Silent night! Holy night!
   Son of God, love's pure light!
   Radiant beams from Thy holy face
   With the dawn of redeeming grace,
   Jesus, Lord at Thy birth,
   Jesus, Lord at Thy birth.

# Index

#7328